& *In memory of Mary Jane Johnson, my mother* &

–V. L. J.

Text and Illustration copyright © 2005 by Marzetta Books

Published by Marzetta Books
P.O. Box 274, Lombard, IL 60148

Printed in Hong Kong

Summary: After one bad hair day, Sarah doesn't feel good about herself. Aunt Lubelle brings soothing comfort, a gentle touch, and ideas for a new hairstyle as Sarah discovers her deep down beauty.

Publisher's Cataloging-in-Publication Data

Johnson, Vincent L.
     Of corn silk and black braids / Vincent Johnson; illustrated by Linda Crockett.— 1st ed.
     p. cm.
     ISBN: 0-9657033-2-0
1. African American girls—Juvenile fiction. 2. Feminine beauty (Aesthetics)—Juvenile fiction.   3. Self-esteem—Juvenile fiction.
4. Self-perception—Juvenile fiction. I. Crockett, Linda. II. Title.

PS3560.O38649 O3 2004
813'.54— dc22

LCCN: 2003116224

Corn Silk and Black Braids

WRITTEN BY VINCENT L. JOHNSON, M.D.

ILLUSTRATED BY LINDA CROCKETT

Marzetta
BOOKS

"Ouch, o-o-ouch! Mama, that hurts!"

"Sarah, I told you not to play out in the rain.
Your hair's always so hard to comb when it gets
wet!"

Sarah sat in a big oak chair, her feet dangling
over the floor. She felt like a prisoner.

The kitchen was usually a pleasant place. But this morning, even though the smells of breakfast still filled the room, Sarah was concerned about her sore head. Her mother pulled a comb through what seemed like a sea of stiff wire, digging down to Sarah's scalp and coming up each time with what looked like a fistful of hair. When the comb passed through Sarah's hair, it sounded like the wind blowing through dry leaves: "Pip, crackle, pop, snap!"

Her mother finished by making two big braids that hung over Sarah's ears. "See, Sarah, all done."

Sarah walked to the bedroom she shared with her younger sister, Maggie, and looked into her mirror. "It's ugly," she said in a low voice. Little strands were sticking from her braids like they had a mind of their own. *If I only had a ribbon or something to make my hair look better,* she thought.

"Sarah, let's get ready to go shopping," her mother called. Unfortunately, Sarah was embarrassed to step out the door.

"Come on, Sarah, your hair looks fine!"

It was a long way to the store. Sarah and her mother stepped along a peaceful country road. Birds cheeped, and the breeze was soothing and cool. The sweet scent of roadside trees tickled Sarah's nose. Occasionally, she would see a caterpillar cross their path. She began to forget about her hair.

As they approached the store, Sarah saw Mrs. Peters and her daughter, Mary Beth. While their mothers talked, Sarah and Mary Beth said hello. Mary Beth's shiny golden hair was covered with beautiful pink ribbons. The wind blew some of Mary Beth's smooth, soft hair across Sarah's face. Sarah wanted to touch it. She leaned toward Mary Beth and slowly lifted her hand, but Mary Beth noticed and moved away.

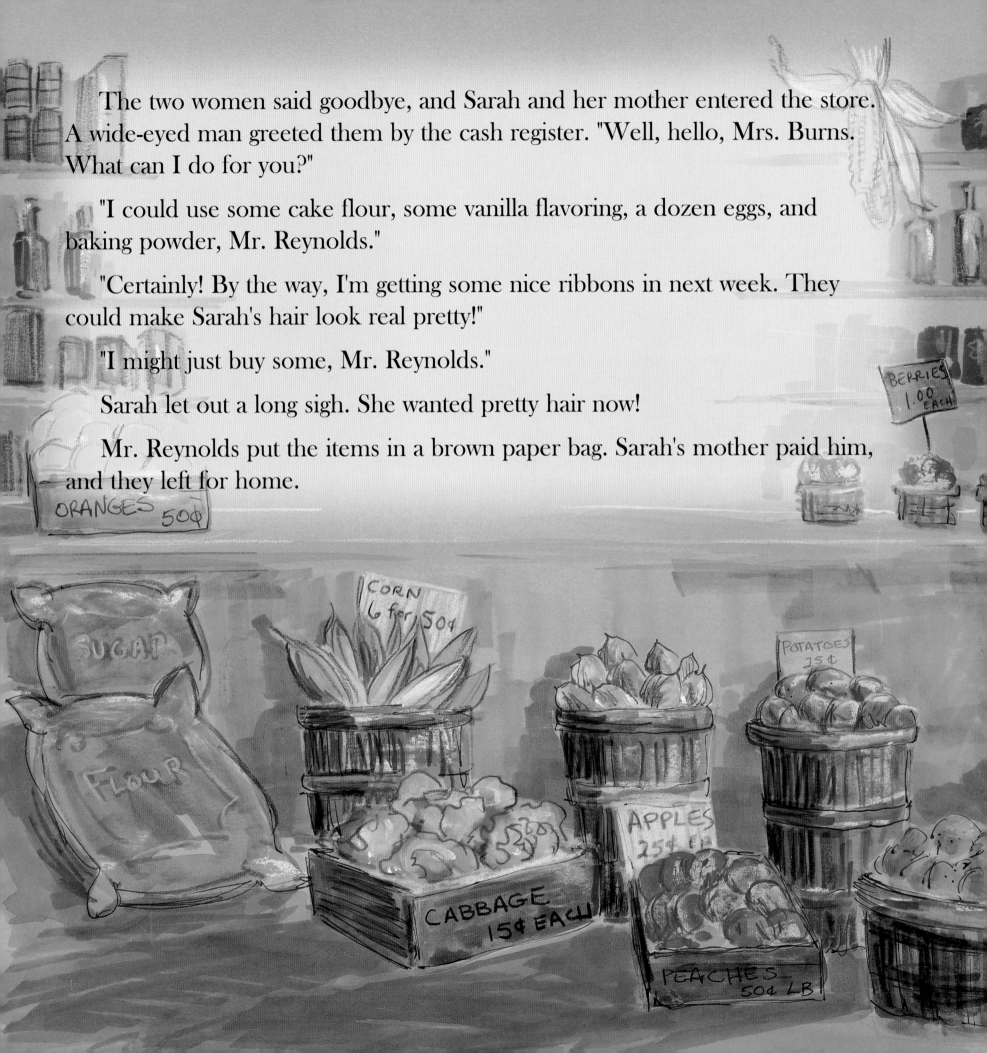

The two women said goodbye, and Sarah and her mother entered the store. A wide-eyed man greeted them by the cash register. "Well, hello, Mrs. Burns. What can I do for you?"

"I could use some cake flour, some vanilla flavoring, a dozen eggs, and baking powder, Mr. Reynolds."

"Certainly! By the way, I'm getting some nice ribbons in next week. They could make Sarah's hair look real pretty!"

"I might just buy some, Mr. Reynolds."

Sarah let out a long sigh. She wanted pretty hair now!

Mr. Reynolds put the items in a brown paper bag. Sarah's mother paid him, and they left for home.

When they arrived, Sarah's mother began to cook dinner.

"Mama, may I go for a walk?"

"All right, but be back before dinner, and don't mess up your hair!"

Sarah ran off as fast as she could, until she came to a large cornfield. She felt short among the tall, green plants. The stringy corn silk glistened in the sun, reminding her of Mary Beth's golden hair. *How could corn silk be so beautiful?* she thought. An ear of corn, its silk sparkling, caught her eye, so she reached up and picked it. She held the ear like a doll, then played with the smooth, soft corn silk as if it were hair. It didn't feel exactly like Mary Beth's, but it was close enough.

When it was near dinnertime, Sarah grabbed a handful of corn silk and ran back to the house, then went to her bedroom. She knew that dinner was about to start, but she just had to play with the corn silk once more. She placed some over her hair, then started dancing around the room, letting the corn silk bounce. When she looked into her mirror, the corn silk glistened almost as much as Mary Beth's hair had done.

"Sarah, dinnertime!" her mother called. Sarah couldn't let her mother see the corn silk, so she quickly put it under the bed. She didn't notice that she still had some on the back of her hair.

When everyone was seated and ready to eat, Maggie noticed the corn silk. She asked, "Sarah, what's that on the back of your head? Did you dye your hair?"

Sarah felt so embarrassed that she didn't know what to say or do. "I didn't put dye on my hair, Maggie!" She tried to say it as softly as possible. She thought that it would help if she left the table as soon as she could, so she ate a little faster.

Then her mother noticed. "Let's see your hair, Sarah. Have you been playing in a cornfield? You know how long it took to do your hair this morning! I want you to get that stuff out of your hair right now!"

"Okay, Mama," Sarah said in a low voice. She went back to her bedroom and removed the corn silk from her hair.

Sarah saw her doll across the room and decided to play with it. She pulled the corn silk, now sort of dry, but still shiny, from under the bed. She put it over her doll's head, saying, "Mama doesn't want me putting corn silk on my hair, but let's see how it looks on you!"

Sarah was surprised at how different her doll looked —sort of cute, she thought— and played with it until bedtime. Maggie came in and got in bed, but didn't go to sleep. Sarah whispered, "Maggie, do you like your hair?"

"It's okay. I don't think about it a lot."

"I mean, do you really like it?" Sarah asked, looking Maggie in the eye. "This morning my hair was all messed up. When Mama and I went to town, Mrs. Peters's daughter had such pretty hair. I tried touching it, and she acted like I had a disease or something."

"If she acted that way with me I wouldn't even wanna touch her old hair!" exclaimed Maggie.

Sarah put some corn silk over her hair again, trying to work it into a hairstyle.

"Oooh, Sarah! If Mama sees you with corn silk in your hair, you're gonna get it!"

"How do you like it, Maggie?"

"Well, I'm sorry, Sarah, but I don't like it."

Sarah looked at Maggie with tears in her eyes. "Why not, Maggie?"

"Well. . . it looks so different!"

Sarah pulled the corn silk from her hair. Just then, their mother slipped into the room.

"What are the two of you doing awake?" Sarah's mother saw the yellow strands in the doll's hair. "I'm going to tuck you in, Maggie. But you come with me to the kitchen, Sarah."

"Mama, is Sarah in trouble?" Maggie asked worriedly.

"Sarah will be fine. Now get to sleep, Maggie."

When they sat down in the kitchen, Sarah wondered what her mother wanted. They hardly ever talked late at night.

"Sarah, did you put corn silk in your doll's hair?"

"Mama, you didn't want the corn silk in my hair, so I put some on my doll."

"Where did you get that idea?"

"Well, this morning Mary Beth's bows were so nice, and her hair was so pretty. I didn't have a bow, but I wanted pretty hair too. And on my walk, I saw all the beautiful corn silk."

"Sarah, do you want blonde hair?"

"Not really, Mama. I just want my hair to be pretty."

Sarah's mother looked at her with a loving smile. "Sarah, I want you to be proud of who you are. You don't have to change yourself to be beautiful. Sometimes your hair is hard to comb, but we just have to work with it until we get a style you like. Now go to bed and think about what I told you."

Sarah went back to her bedroom. She lay thinking about Mary Beth's hair, the brilliant corn silk and how it had looked on her and her doll. Eventually, she fell asleep.

The next day was beautiful. It was special because Aunt Lubelle, a tall, sassy African American woman who wore colorful dresses, was coming to visit. Lubelle was Sarah's favorite aunt, so when she arrived, they hugged each other very tightly. Aunt Lubelle noticed Sarah's hair.

"Sylvia, what have you done to my baby?"

"What are you talking about?" Sarah's mother replied.

"This hair, Sylvia!"

Aunt Lubelle ran her soothing hands over Sarah's head.

"Lubelle, she played in the rain. I did my best!"

"You weren't ever good at fixing hair, Sylvia. Come on, Sarah, I'll fix your hair. Let's go on the porch."

Aunt Lubelle carefully unbraided Sarah's hair.

"Sarah, you're a pretty young lady."

"Aunt Lubelle, sometimes I hate my hair. Yesterday, Mama and I went to town, and I saw the most beautiful golden hair."

"Sarah, your hair is nice, too. Anyway, my favorite girl doesn't have to look at anyone else's hair thinking that it's so pretty and her own isn't!"

"Well, it looked really nice, and my hair hasn't ever looked that way."

"Sarah, you were born with special hair! It can be made into all kinds of styles."

"Aunt Lubelle, you should see Mary Beth. She has good hair."

Aunt Lubelle looked at Sarah's hair, then held her hand. "There's no such thing as pretty or ugly or good or bad hair. It's what you do with it. Let's see what we can do. How about Aunt Lubelle's special braids?"

Sarah didn't know what to think. "Okay, I guess," she said softly. *But Mary Beth didn't have braids,* she thought.

Aunt Lubelle made five small braids on each side of Sarah's head. They danced whenever Sarah moved.

"What do you think of this, Sarah?"

Sarah ran to peek into the mirror. "It's okay, but it could look a little better," she said. Aunt Lubelle took down Sarah's hair and started over. This time, she made three larger braids on each side and added a cute little bang.

When Sarah looked this time, all the strands seemed to be in place. It was the best hairstyle she'd ever had. She began to feel better about her hair, but it still didn't look as good as she wanted it to, so she ran back to the porch.

Aunt Lubelle worked late into the afternoon. *Just what is going to please Sarah?* she wondered and thought of yet another style to try. It was almost dinnertime. Her fingers ached.

When she was finished, Sarah jumped up and ran to the mirror. At first she was afraid to look. What if she didn't like this hairstyle either? She couldn't ask her aunt for another one!

Sarah cautiously took a peek. Her head was covered with braids in little rows hugging her scalp from front to back and then hanging down to her shoulders. The beautiful cornrows were much prettier than corn silk! Sarah was really surprised. Her hair wasn't golden, and she wasn't wearing any ribbons, but her hair was so beautiful!

Sarah jumped for joy. She was so happy that she ran to show everyone what a beautiful job Aunt Lubelle had done, then ran back to the porch and exclaimed, "I really like it, Auntie!" She hugged and squeezed Aunt Lubelle.

"Sarah, I just wanted you to be happy with your hair."

The next day Aunt Lubelle planned to go shopping and asked Sarah to come along. During their long walk, they talked about everything except hair. But Sarah couldn't stop thinking about her cornrows.

As they approached town, Sarah saw Mary Beth and her mother. "That's Mary Beth, Auntie."

Aunt Lubelle and Mrs. Peters began talking. Mary Beth immediately noticed Sarah's hairstyle. "Hi, Sarah. What kind of hairstyle do you have?"

"They're cornrows, my Aunt Lubelle's special braids."

"They're braids? They're pretty!"

"Yes, it took all afternoon to do my hair."

"It takes a lot of work to do my hair, too. My mother talks about cutting it shorter," Mary Beth replied. Sarah had had no idea that Mary Beth had problems with her hair, too.

When they got home, Sarah told Aunt Lubelle what Mary Beth had said. Aunt Lubelle touched Sarah's cheek. "Sarah, I wasn't trying to make you beautiful, because you already are. I just fixed your hair so that you could see the beauty that's there inside you!"

Sarah stared at herself in the mirror, grinning from ear to ear. She thought about the last two days. Yes, golden hair could bounce and shine beautifully. Ribbons and bows made hair look beautiful, too.

But even the caterpillars in the road had beautiful little hairs sticking up from their backs. She giggled when she imagined caterpillars getting their hair done. She realized that beautiful things came in different shapes and sizes. Most important of all, she began to discover her own beauty, her deep down beauty.

Sarah gazed deeply into her reflection. *I am beautiful,* she thought.